# DIARY OF A
# NINJA
# SPY

*Where evil goes, the ninja will follow…*

*Diary of a Ninja Spy  (Book 1)*

*William Thomas*

*Peter Patrick*

*For Ethan, Chelsea and Sophie.*

# Chapter 1

Oh, the life of a sixth grader.

I know what you're thinking – life should be all fun, parties and laughs at this age. But it's not.

School is boring as. Totally.

Except for the day when Martin's shorts kept falling down. That wasn't boring.

That was funny.

But, usually, the most excitement we get is when we listen to the story of the Evil Shadow attacking on television. He is the world's scariest, meanest, and most elusive ninja!

WANTED
EVIL
NINJA

Even though this mysterious ninja is evil, I think he is *sooo* cool. There is something about his story that has drawn me in.

The Evil Shadow has been making his way around the world attacking random things and vandalizing monuments, while searching for something.

About two months ago, he took the Big Ben clock tower in London and made it Little Ben.

He painted the Statue of Liberty bright yellow while New York City slept.

Even the Sydney Opera House in Australia was turned upside down.

One of his most bizarre and astonishing feats was the relocation of Mt Everest!

It now sits on a small island in the Pacific Ocean.

Totally weird.

Every country in the world is searching for him now. You would think with everyone looking, somebody would see something. But nope. Nothing. Nada. Not a thing.

The ninja is a master of disappearing.

I wish something that exciting would happen in our town. Nothing exciting ever happens here.

My name is Blake Turner and I am eleven years old.

As you can tell, I've been working out – I've been pumping iron and am full of muscle.

This is me.

And this is my best friend, Fred.

As you can see, we are not the coolest kids in school.

"Blake! Blake!" Fred runs up to me after class finishes for the day.

"Hey Fred. What's up?"

"Did you see the new story about the Evil Shadow?" he puffs after running down the hallway.

"No, I haven't. Anything interesting?"

"Well, check this out!"

Fred pulls out his latest high-tech phone and shows me a video of the Evil Shadow attacking a shopping center a few miles away from my house.

"Whoa! That's so awesome!" I shout. "We've got to go there!"

"No way!" Fred argues. "That's totally dangerous!"

"And that's exactly why we should go!"

"No way, man. Look, it isn't the full story either. There isn't just one ninja anymore, now there are over twenty bad ninjas! There is no way we should go! It's dangerous."

"But you could get a great selfie with the Evil Shadow in the background…" I try to convince Fred to go chase the action.

Fred loves a good selfie.

He's got a selfie with the Pyramids, the Eiffel Tower, and the White House. Of course, that was before the Evil Shadow changed them.

But my favorite selfie was when a monkey threw poo at Fred.

That was a classic.

Fred rips out his selfie stick from his pocket!

"Wow! A selfie with the Evil Shadow! Why didn't I think of that?"

"Because you're terrified of ninjas."

"Oh, yeah…"

"Get that selfie stick and let's go!" I yell as I run down the hallway.

*This may turn out to be a very bad idea…*

# Chapter 2

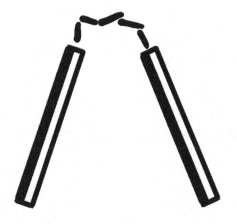

As soon as I get home, I tell my parents that I need a new Math textbook from the local shopping mall.

My Mom goes into shock.

I have never, ever, ever asked for anything to do with school before.

But anything to do with my education always gets top priority and is a sure way of getting me closer to the action.

In excitement, Mom drives me to the car park of the mall, and straight away, we can see the destruction.

Jumping out of the car, I see Fred is already there, taking a selfie.

"Whoa!" I gasp.

I look at the pile of concrete, hardly recognizing it as the shopping mall. The mall has been reshaped into a ten-story concrete tower!

It looks like a lighthouse with all the shops stacked on top of each other.

Totes epic.

Hundreds of police officers, fireman and customers are surrounding the tower. Some of the customers are even climbing down and running away.

I have never seen anything like it!!

"Oh, why does this have to happen today?" Mom moans. "The only day that Blake shows an interest in his school work. It doesn't look like we'll be able to get your much-needed textbook today, son."

"Mom, stop. Stop! Look!" I exclaim, pointing at the tower.

At the top of the tower, I see the Evil Shadow for the first time…

# Chapter 3

The Evil Shadow is so totally cool.

He's standing on top of the large concrete tower, looking for something…

And then he sees me. He stares straight at me…

It's as if he recognizes me!

I freeze.

Like absolutely freeze, the same as a frozen pizza.

I know it was my idea to get closer to the action, but I don't want to be *part* of the action.

"Blake, the Evil Shadow!" yells Fred. "Look up there, it's him. This was an awesome idea!"

My Mom stares at me. "What idea was that, Blake? Hmmmm?"

"Um… to get a new Math textbook today." I don't cover up my story very well, and I'm sure that Mom doesn't believe me.

"Shhh!" whispers Fred. "The Evil Shadow is saying something!"

We listen closely and hear the Evil Shadow starting to yell something – and then…

Wow!

Lots of ninjas start jumping out of the base of the tower!

Everyone begins to panic and run away – even the police officers.

This is so totally wild.

"Blake…? Blake! Can you see that?!" Fred is asking if I can see what he sees.

"I can see it, Fred," I reply without taking my eyes off a girl being kidnapped by a ninja.

A ninja has swooped down on a rope and grabbed a girl, and has taken her back up to the top of the tower.

**Oh no!**

It's Emily - my sixth-grade crush.

Sure, she doesn't know I exist, but I sure know she does.

We talk occasionally, but it's mainly because we have to. We're in a lot of the same classes. We played hide and seek together once when we were younger, and she did a great job of hiding.

I didn't see her again until the next summer.

Once Emily reaches the top, she stops screaming. The ninja hands her over to the Evil Shadow.

I don't think these ninjas are so cool anymore. In fact, I've completely changed my mind; I don't like these guys at all.

"Citizens!" A booming voice says from the top of the tower. "I have one question for you!"

This time, everybody freezes.

"I am seeking an artifact. It is a very important item. It is something I lost generations ago. If I do not receive the item, I will destroy your town," the Evil Shadow declares in a very stern voice. "I seek… the Power Sword!"

"The Power Sword?" I whisper to Fred.

"Yeah, Blake, the Power Sword. You know the one," says Fred, confidently.

"No, I don't. What is it?"

"No idea. Never heard of it."

"I will keep destroying landmarks until my request has been satisfied," the Evil Shadow continues. "I will also start taking hostages, starting with this little girl."

Fred and I stand there amongst the chaos.

"I'm going up there," I say to Fred.

"What? Are you cray-cray? No – don't answer that. I know you're crazy. But tell me why?" asks Fred.

"Because if I don't, nobody else will," I say as I look at the hundreds of people who are fleeing the scene.

"Give me your selfie stick."

Fred nervously hands it over.

With the stick in my hand, I charge towards the mayhem.

I hear my Mom scream out, but I ignore her. This could be a really dumb idea, trying to fight an experienced crafty ninja.

But deep inside, I have a good feeling about this...

# Chapter 4

To get to Emily, my first task is to somehow get past the ninjas that surround the base of the tower. Sneaking up to the mess that used to be the mall, I glance at the first shop sign, 'The Spy and Gadget Shop.'

Perfect!

Running into the store, I look for something, anything, which will help me.

Yes!

On the ground in front of me is a bag that says – 'Spy Pack.' I also grab some fireworks, a pillow, and a can of hair spray.

Sneaking up as close as I can to the base of the tower, I look for the first ninja to attack.

I shove the fireworks into the pillow, together with the can of hair spray, and race towards one of the ninjas.

"Hiiii-Ya!" I scream, with the lit pillow over my shoulder. I throw it at the ninja, who has not moved at all since the beginning of my attack.

In fact, I think he's smirking.

Is he laughing at me?

Does he think I'm no threat at all?

With the pillow gliding through the air, he quickly says to me, "Hiyah? Nobody says hiyah. That's only something ninjas scream out in movies…"

Before he can finish his sentence, the pillow explodes in a bright blue flash!

Yes!

The ninja is dazed.

I jump and use his head as a step to get up to the pile of shops.

I bolt up the side of the tower towards Emily.

Time to be a hero…

# Chapter 5

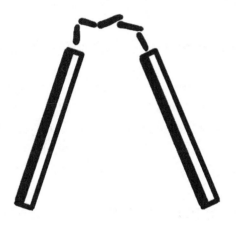

Just before I reach the top of the building, I check what else I have in my spy kit. A glue gun, a tripwire, and a mirror.

Not much of a spy kit – I must have grabbed the cheap one.

Once I'm at the top of the building, I peer cautiously over the edge. I can see Emily tied to a pillar and the Evil Shadow pacing back and forth, waiting. Quietly, I set up a trap.

"Where is my Power Sword? I can sense that you are somehow close to it," the Evil Shadow demands of his captive.

"No, get away from me you pajama man!" replies Emily.

"These are not pajamas! This is an elite ninja uniform!" explains the Evil Shadow.

"They sure look like jam jams to me!" I state as I climb onto the rooftop.

What a great entrance!

That should be in a movie.

"Who are you?" asks the startled Evil Shadow, "How did I not hear you creep up on me? Nobody can creep up on me…"

As he is blubbering away, I quickly whip out the mirror from my spy pack and shine it on his face.

Blinded by the reflection of the sunlight, the Evil Shadow stumbles forward towards the tripwire I had set up.

Just as he trips over, I pull out my instant glue gun and spray his feet with it!

Yes!

He sticks to the rooftop!

Man, I am awesome sometimes.

"Hey. I'm stuck!" he yells. "How did you do this? I am the great ninja! I cannot be fooled!"

"Whatever man," I reply. "Maybe you're not so great after all."

The Evil Shadow then pulls out a set of nunchucks!

But I can't get to Emily unless I get past him first.

Even with his feet glued to the ground, the Evil Shadow is throwing his weapon around with full force.

I duck and weave, trying to get past to rescue Emily.

I reach into my back pocket and pull out my secret weapon - Fred's selfie stick.

He swings his nunchucks – I duck!

Yes!

I swing the selfie stick – he dodges it!

This is totally the best battle ever.

Then I put together a combination of sweet ninja moves. Left-arm swing, right-arm swing… and then right-leg kick!

It works and the Evil Shadow is disarmed!

His nunchucks go flying away from him.

"What?! I recognize those ninjutsu skills! Where did you learn those moves?!" he demands. "Tell me!"

"I simply made them up," I reply with a smile.

"Impossible, those are rare and ancient techniques you displayed. No one knows those traditional moves. They have not been used in centuries," questions the Evil Shadow.

"Gasp…unless…" the Evil Shadow looks puzzled, but then quickly dismisses it. "No, no, impossible!"

I don't listen to him any further and scurry past to untie Emily before we retreat down the tower.

"See ya, glue feet!" I yell.

I realize as we run away it was a stupid thing to say – I so should have said something funnier!

# Chapter 6

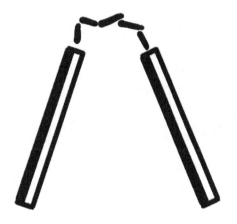

As we make our way down the tower, we can see the other ninjas retreating.

I think Emily is very impressed with my heroic actions. "Thank you so much, ….um…"

"Blake. My name is Blake," I say. Surely she knew that already. It must be the shock that has made her forget my name.

"How can I ever repay you, Blake?" she asks.

"Your safety is enough reward for me."

Aw man, what a cheesy thing to say!

When we arrive at the bottom of the tower, Fred is waiting for us.

"Wow, Blake! That was incredible. You never told me you practiced martial arts!" he screams in excitement.

"I don't know any martial arts. I was just trying not to get sliced in two. It all just happened naturally."

"That's totes cool. I got some great photos from down here. I even got a selfie with the Evil Shadow in the background," claims Fred. "You are so brave, Blake! Isn't he the bravest, Emily?"

"By far the bravest guy I know. But I had the situation under control. Two more minutes and I would've freed myself," remarks Emily.

She is probably right - Emily is known for being one of the toughest students in the whole state. She has a black belt in karate and once tied a group of eagles together that were trying to take her lunch.

Emily moves closer to me and holds my hand. "But I'm still grateful that you rescued me."

Oh man… this day could not get any better!

"BLAKE! Get back here now!"

Eek! That's my Mom screaming out from the car park.

I'm so doomed.

"Not so brave now, are you?" laughs Fred, seeing the fear on my face.

The three of us start to walk back towards my Mom's car... when suddenly a short fizz ignites and a puff of smoke appears right in front of us!

Once it clears, we see another ninja standing there.

Oh, no!

I instinctively push the others behind me.

Usually, I would be excited to come face to face with a ninja, but after the last experience I've lost my enthusiasm.

"What do you want?" I demand of the ninja.

"I mean you no harm," states the ninja, bowing to me. "I am here as a friend. I am not associated with those ninjas you just encountered. I have just arrived here with my colleagues."

"Who are you? Who are your colleagues?"

"Are you familiar with the ninja and his henchmen you just met?" he asks.

Fred speaks up. "Yeah, we call him the Evil Shadow. The others were part of his gang."

"My team of ninjas and I are trying to capture him. My name is Tekato."

"Teeto?" repeats Fred.

"No. Tekato."

"Oh, Teaaa-kato," says Fred.

"No. Tekato."

"Ohhh, right. Te-kito."

"No. Tekato."

"Oh, yes. Yes, I get it now," says Fred again. "Teeekaaattttooooooo."

"No! Tekato!"

"Alright, ninja-man. No need to get angry. How's this – Tekata?"

The ninja shakes his head. "Grrrr....you can just call me 'Ninja.'"

"Cool. Thanks, Mr. Ninjo."

The ninja looks *really* angry now.

"So, you're a good ninja?" asks Emily from behind my shoulder, stopping the silly conversation from going any further.

"Yes, I am part of an organization whose mission is to keep the Evil Shadow and his gang from destroying the world," says the ninja, standing to attention.

"The agency?" I cut in. "The Ninja Spy Agency?! Does it really exist? I heard rumors, but I thought they were just myths."

"Those rumors are true," confirms the ninja. "I am from a world of espionage and action."

"Whoa!" I yell.

"We keep our presence secret, and most people don't know we exist. We are the most elite ninjas and spies on earth. It takes years of hard training and lots of dedication to join our organization," explains Tekato.

"So, what are you doing here? Are you going to stop the Evil Shadow?" asks Emily.

"We have been trying to stop him for many centuries. But he is too skillful at the art of disappearing."

"Whoa! What? Centuries? That's, like, a super long time."

Tekato stands tall. "Three hundred years ago in Japan, all the ninjas fought for a common goal. All ninjas vowed to protect our land from the dangers of a local dragon, the Magical Mountain Serpent. A promising young ninja, who was overly fond of greatness, decided to steal a dragon egg from the Magical Mountain Serpent."

"Wow," I gasp. "A real dragon?"

"Yes, a real dragon that still lives today," continues the masked man. "The young ninja was told by his friends to leave the egg alone, but he wanted to impress his local village with his loot. The village knew that the mother dragon would not be as impressed. And they were right. While the boy showed his prize to his village friends, the mother of the egg found him. Scared of the dragon, the boy dropped the egg and it broke."

"That poor baby dragon!" exclaims Emily.

The ninja does not stop to console Emily. "The mother dragon cursed the boy to live forever and destroyed the village. That cursed young man was called the Evil Shadow. He recruited others who had aspired to be ninjas but failed. The Evil Shadow went on to build an army of destructive ninjas and is now intent on destroying the world."

"When he was holding me hostage, he was asking me about a Power Sword?" asks Emily.

"This is what he is searching for. The Power Sword is thousands of years old and is the key to ending this madness," snaps the ninja. "The Power Sword was crafted from the remains of the broken dragon's egg by the Evil Shadow. It contains a magic power that is almost unimaginable. It can cause great damage in a single strike. The sword was lost many years ago in a battle with the Ninjutsu Grand Master, a former agent of the Ninja Spy Agency. If it falls into the hands of the Evil Shadow, he could destroy mankind."

Emily's eyes widen. "Can just anyone use the sword?"

"No. Only the Evil Shadow himself... but there is a myth that one person per generation can handle the Power Sword, and they are known as the Chosen One. If the sword falls into the hands of the Chosen One, they may be able to defeat the Evil Shadow and end this madness," says the ninja.

"So, who is the Chosen One?" I ask.

"Nobody knows. In fact, even the Chosen One probably doesn't know."

The ninja turns to me. "Blake, nobody has ever captured the Evil Shadow before."

"How did you know my name?" I question him.

"I was standing next to your Mom in the car park when she was screaming at you on top of the tower. You are in big trouble, buddy." He laughs. "But before I disappear, here is a picture of the Power Sword. Keep this in mind and if you ever see it, contact the Ninja Spy Agency."

The good ninja spy shows me a picture of the Power Sword on his smartphone.

"Gee, even ninjas have phones now," remarks Fred.

"Well, I have friends too, you know," scoffs Tekato. "Everybody just assumes ninjas don't have social lives, pfft."

While the phone is passed around, Fred says, "I'll be your friend, Teto."

"My name is not Teto! My name is Tekato!"

Emily rolls her eyes. "Let's just move on from the name please."

"Excuse me, Tekato?"

"Yes, Blake."

"I have a sword like that in my shed – it was a present from some random guy dressed as Santa when I was three years old..."

# Chapter 7

After Mom gives me a lecture about being too dangerous, we arrive back at my house and I run straight to the garden shed.

Where is that sword?

I dig through some old boxes and junk before I finally find it!

"Here it is. It's been just sitting here with a box of old toys," I say to myself as I point to the sword.

Tekato appears again out of nowhere and checks out the sword.

"Whoa, man, where did you come from?" I ask in surprise.

"The shadows…" he says in a mysterious voice.

"The shadows?"

"Oh yeah – I just hitched a ride on the back of your car and waited in the shadows until you arrived."

"Oh."

"Hheeee," stresses Tekato as he tries to pick up the sword. "Is this a cruel joke? I can't lift it. It is stuck to the floor."

"Haha, it's only a toy sword, you weakling! I used to play with it all day long when I was three," I say.

I step forward and pick it up with ease. Tekato looks stunned and turns to me.

"Blake," he says.

"Yo, Ninja Bro."

"I think you may be the Chosen One…"

# Chapter 8

"Blake, this is unbelievable. You must be the Chosen One," whispers Tekato as we stand in my garden shed. "We have searched for someone like you for decades. It is an honor to be in your presence."

Tekato bows towards me.

"Cool man," I shrug.

"Do you understand what we have to do next?" asks Tekato.

"Ahhh…" I reply. I know the answer, but I'm not sure if I can get approval from Mom to go and save the world.

"Are you worried about what your mother is going to say?"

"Well, yes. Yes, I am. I really want to help, Tekato. But if I can't get permission to leave the house, I'll be no help at all," I state.

"I will simply use my convincing potion on her," says Tekato as he hurries me back towards the house.

"Mom?" I ask when I walk in through the backdoor with Tekato next to me.

Immediately, as Mom turns around, Tekato throws pink dust in her face.

Mom carries on as if nothing happened.

"Ask her," prompts Tekato.

"Ah, Mom, this is my new friend, Tekato."

Mom is going to go berserk. I'm standing in the house with a ninja who clearly has a lot of sharp and unsafe weapons.

I'm *sooo* dead!

"Hello, Tekato. How are you?" asks Mom like there's no problem at all.

What?! No reaction? Did that potion really work?

Ninja's are so cool.

"Mom, Tekato and I are going to go back to the mall where the Evil Shadow attacked today. I have the ability to control a thing called the Power Sword. I'm going to have a sword fight to defeat the most dangerous person on earth, and save the world," I nervously tell her.

"Sure, dear. Have fun," replies Mom without even raising an eyebrow. "Just be home by dinner time."

I turn to Tekato and whisper, "What? Did that really work?"

"Sure did. Now, we must go."

Together, we race back to the shopping center where we last saw the Evil Shadow. But there's a major problem - the entire scene is now swamped with TV reporters and police officers.

"To get up to the top of the tower we need to use some classic disguises," says Tekato as he points to a TV news van.

"Awesome, I've always wanted to be a cameraman," I say as I grab a camera from the van.

"I'll disguise myself as a policeman. If anyone asks what we are doing, our explanation is that I'm escorting you to the top of the crime scene."

Tekato sneaks up to a police motorbike and takes the bike helmet. He slips it on and covers the most suspicious thing about him, his masked head.

I wonder what he looks like under the ninja mask?

He waves me through the police tape and we enter the crime scene without any questions.

"That seemed too easy," I say to Tekato as we climb the stack of shops.

"As a ninja, it is important to be able to disappear into one's surroundings," Tekato responds. "In the past I've disguised myself as an old woman, a horse, a car, a lamp, and a large poo. Being able to disguise yourself is a very important part of being a ninja."

"I once disguised myself as a gorilla to score some free bananas. Is that the same thing?" I ask.

"No, no it is not," says Tekato in a no-nonsense tone.

As we get closer to the top, I grip the Power Sword tight. I'm a little anxious about battling a three-hundred-year-old ninja, even if his feet are still stuck to the ground.

"Are you ready to battle with the most dangerous person on earth, Blake?" asks Tekato.

"Meh," I shrug, not showing any fear.

"Remember Blake, use the Power Sword. You need to defeat him," reminds Tekato.

We reach the top of the building…

"No!"

Only the Evil Shadow's boots remain glued to the roof…

# Chapter 9

I go to school the next day as if nothing has changed.

But in fact, everything has changed.

I could potentially save the world and stop the Evil Shadow's madness.

We looked for the Evil Shadow for a while after we arrived at the mall, but we couldn't find him. Tekato told me not to worry – he will be back… and most likely hunt me down.

He also told me it is very important that I stay undetected. I am not to tell anyone that I am the 'Chosen One.'

The time will come when I need to battle the Evil Shadow again.

Until then, I must keep the sword close by so that it doesn't fall into the wrong hands. The Evil Shadow's team of ninja spies may be hiding close by.

I asked Tekato if I'm just bait to trap the Evil Shadow, but he assured me I am completely safe.

Right now, I'm carrying the sword in my school bag, and just to test the theory of its uncontrollable power, I ask Fred to handle the sword.

"Go on, Fred," I say. "I want you to catch this."

"Is this some trick?" he responds. "I really want to tell everybody about what happened last night! It was the most incredible experience of my life!"

"No, we can't, Fred. We made a promise to Tekato and we should honor it."

"Well, what about Emily? You did hold hands with her! Your biggest crush!" continues Fred.

I smile and nod. "Look, just catch the sword."

I take the sword out of my backpack and focus hard on it. When I start to feel something, I throw it to Fred to catch. The sword does not disappoint.

Suddenly a bright blue glow appears and the sword is flying and darting around the room. Fred literally can't control its power.

"Ahhh!" yells Fred.

"Fred, let go of the sword!" I yell back.

Fred does – but as he does, he is thrown across the room into a pile of schoolbags.

"What just happened? I couldn't even hold it, it had a life of its own!" says Fred, stunned.

I pick it up with ease again as if it's a hollow, plastic toy.

"Fred," I say. "I need to tell you something… I am the Chosen One."

"OMG!"

"This sword can only be controlled by myself and the Evil Shadow. It is also the only weapon that can completely stop the Evil Shadow," I explain. "Not even the ninjas from the spy agency can control it. But I must keep the sword safe and away from the Evil Shadow."

"Whoa," gasps Fred.

"I promised not to tell anyone so keep your mouth shut. Okay?" I say to Fred as I realize my mistake.

But I had to tell somebody!

I couldn't keep a secret like that to myself!

I put the Power Sword in my locker and make my way to class. But class is with Miss Pineapple – the world's most boring science teacher. How does someone make blowing things up seem boring?

Soon, I'm daydreaming out the window instead of listening to her story about science in the 1950s.

What? That's odd. I just saw a shadow flash across the glass.

Then another shadow…

And then another!

This is not normal, and I have a feeling this is related to my sword.

"Miss Pineapple! I need to go to the toilet," I yell out.

The classroom erupts in laughter.

"Blake! Raise your hand if you would like to ask something. Do not just yell out in my classroom. Understood?" she says, looking cross with me.

Man, this is embarrassing, but I need to get to the sword in my locker. Quick!

"I have to go! I'm going to wee myself!" I make an excuse as I jump up and run to the door. No doubt Miss Pineapple is upset, but she isn't going to argue with me now.

The classrooms attention quickly diverts from me to the growing amount of shadows darting around the room.

The ninjas are back, and I don't think they're the good ones either...

# Chapter 10

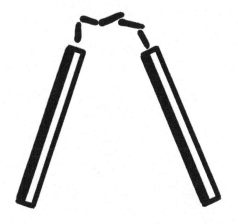

I charge down the empty hallway to get to my locker, only to lose my footing and slide into a corner.

All the corridors in the school are covered with some kind of oil. I slip and slide everywhere trying to stand up.

I can't control where I'm going!

Lying, soaked in oil, I get a glimpse of a ninja looking around.

It isn't the Evil Shadow I met yesterday, but he doesn't look like a friendly one either. It must be one of the Evil Shadow's army!

I push myself off a wall and slide at full speed towards the skinny ninja's legs. Good move!

I quickly bowl him over and as he lies there in shock, I quickly whip off the non-slip boots he's wearing.

After I put my shoes straight into his boots, I move towards my locker. I look around - no sign of any other ninjas.

My plan is to get the sword out of here and as far away from the school as possible. Hopefully, the Ninja Spy agents will come to my aid soon!

Just as I open my locker and grasp the sword, a hand comes over my shoulder.

It grabs the sword from my locker!

No!

Not the Power Sword!

There is only one hand other than mine that can grab it…

The Evil Shadow!

I take a quick look at him.

Why doesn't he have new boots yet? I guess ninja boots must be hard to find.

"This sword belongs to me," says the Evil Shadow.

"Give it back, it's mine!" I yell.

"Really?" he replies in a sarcastic tone.

"Yes, really. Let go, it's my sword! It was given to me!"

"I made this sword hundreds of years ago, it belongs to me," repeats the Evil Shadow. "This sword is my last obstacle to destroying the world. I shall have it," he states. "Besides, how can you handle its power?"

He pauses for a second. "Wait, could you be… you did pull some pretty smooth moves on me before," he whispers to himself.

I need to distract him so I can lunge at the sword. I go to my secret weapon – my jokes.

"Knock knock," I say.

The Evil Shadow sighs. "Who's there?"

"Sam."

"Sam who?"

"Sam-urai!" I yell as I make my move.

But he didn't even laugh – boy, this ninja is serious!

I focus all my energy on getting control of the sword and I dive at the handle.

Suddenly we are both hanging onto the sword!

Bring it on!

"I am the Chosen One! I can handle the Power Sword. You have met your match now, Evil Shadow!" I announce with determination.

"But can you do this?" questions the Evil Shadow.

I look straight at the Evil Shadow while fighting for control of the sword.

"Do what?" I ask.

Suddenly a huge blast shoots out from the Power Sword.

*Damn…*

# Chapter 11

The blast from the sword sends me flying across the corridor.

I smash into a row of lockers, and man, it hurts!

A lot.

Once I pick myself off the floor, I rush at the Power Sword again, hoping to simply grab it off him.

But he turns too fast and flips me over the top of him.

This time, I crash into the wall outside my English classroom. I get up again, shake off my daze and make another rush at him… and he does the same again.

I am clearly out-skilled here, a professional ninja against a schoolboy.

How can I win this?

Every move I make, he easily counteracts. My fighting technique is not coming as naturally to me as it did with the selfie stick.

Suddenly, the Evil Shadow floats into the air.

Unbelievable!

"Can you do this with the sword? No, you cannot," says the floating Evil Shadow. "I can harness the magic of the Power Sword! You can only touch it. I can unleash its true potential. You do not appreciate this weapon. This gift is wasted on you."

While I'm on the ground, I grab a heap of objects from the broken lockers and fling them at him like ninja stars.

First, I launch a ruler, then a pencil case, then a textbook, followed by a lunch box and a rotten fish… Uh!

Who keeps a rotten fish in their locker? Oh wait, that must be Rotten Fish Jimmy. That would explain his nickname.

All five objects are deflected by his sword, but I see my chance to attack!

I leap straight up as the Evil Shadow comes towards me with the sword.

Uh-oh.

This is my worst move so far…

The Evil Shadow lowers his body and perfects a sweep-kick on me.

I never stood a chance.

"Give me back my sword!" I scream as I'm flipped in the air again.

I want my toy back. And only for the same reason any kid wants their toy back - someone else is playing with it.

I'm lying, beaten, on the ground in front of him and all my moves have failed.

"Are you prepared for your defeat, young man? It will be my honor to slice open the Chosen One."

I look around and see all his ninja goons watching me.

The Evil Shadow moves into another attacking stance.

*Oh no…*

*I'm doomed…*

# Chapter 12

*Zzzzooom.*

**Click.**

Huh? What?

It's Fred!

Fred has taken a selfie with me in the background about to be demolished by the Evil Shadow. Yep, thanks Fred. What a good memory that will be.

But the camera has caught the Evil Shadow off guard!

He's distracted by the flash…

And that's all I need!

This is it, my moment to knock him out.

I launch straight up.

It's go time!

As we wrestle in the air, I'm able to get one hand on the sword.

I hold onto it, tight.

Come on!

I squeeze the sword harder.

And focus.

I want to unleash the blast from the sword!

Come on! Blast already!

We land on the ground together, still with the sword handle in my grip, and I look at the Evil Shadow.

"I am the Chosen One," I say. "You are Evil. And I am here to send evil home."

Wow – I really should have practiced my threatening statements.

But just after I say it, a powerful, electric force surges from my hand and onto the sword.

# Boom!!

Yes!

The blast blows the Evil Shadow through a window at lightning speed. Wow! I can harness the energy of the Power Sword!

I charge towards the window to land my final blast, but the Evil Shadow is gone...

Along with his henchman ninjas.

There isn't a sound in the whole hallway.

They have retreated.

I have beaten them.

Awesome!

# Epilogue

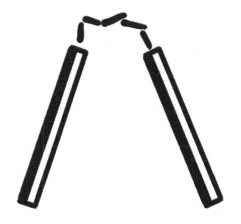

Teachers and kids run and slide as they enter the hallway to see what was making all the noise.

"What is going on here?!" yells Miss Pineapple. "Have you been to the toilet yet, Blake?"

I really want to tell all of them what just happened, but I quickly remember what Tekato told me.

A ninja must keep his identity secret.

And I *so* want to become a real ninja.

Therefore, I must remain in the shadows as a humble hero.

"Not yet, Miss. I still need to wee," I tell her.

Ahh, just great. I just saved the planet only to totally humiliate myself in front of everyone.

"And get rid of your toy sword too, Blake. If I find out you broke that window and made this mess, you are in big trouble!" continues Miss Pineapple. "Everyone else, stop laughing and get back to class!"

I want to tell the teacher that my 'toy sword' was actually a magical sword created hundreds of years ago and only I can control it!

But I can't.

As I turn around to walk to the bathroom, Tekato appears in front of me.

"Where is he? Have we come too late?" he asks.

"I beat him and he ran off," I say, quite proud of myself.

I finally get to tell someone.

Yes!

"You beat him?"

"Sure did," I smile.

"Congratulations. If you have beaten him then his stamina will be damaged by the Power Sword. He will not return for some time. I believe you have a future," says Tekato.

"Thanks, I am only young and I do eat healthy sometimes," I reply.

"No, a future with us, the Ninja Spy Agency," he states, looking serious.

"Really? You mean, I can become a Ninja Spy?".

I've always wanted to be a Ninja Spy.

Well, at least since I found out about their existence yesterday.

"Can I get a cool ninja name, maybe something like Doomsday Blake or Blake the Ninja Assassin?" I ask.

"Your name is not important at the moment, Blake," says Tekato. "However, your training is. I will be your Sensei. You will need to survive intense training and you need a haircut. But I have faith in you. You show great promise. The world needs ninja spies more than ever, even if nobody knows it."

He hands me a uniform.

"Try it on, and let me know your decision," says Tekato.

I put it on quickly.

"Blake, are you willing to take an oath and dedicate your life to upholding the mission of the Ninja Spy Agency?"

I put on the mask and consider what he has just asked...

"Yes, Tekato. Yes, I am."

# The End

*Also in the Diary of a Ninja Spy series:*

**Diary of a Ninja Spy 2**

**Diary of a Ninja Spy 3**

**Diary of a Ninja Spy 4**

**Diary of a Ninja Spy 5**

*Also by William Thomas and Peter Patrick:*

**Diary of a Super Spy**

**Diary of a Super Spy 2: Attack of the Ninjas!**

**Diary of a Super Spy 3: A Giant Problem!**

**Diary of a Super Spy 4: Space!**

**Diary of a Super Spy 5: Evil Attack!**

**Diary of a Super Spy 6: Daylight Robbery**

Made in the USA
Coppell, TX
22 January 2020